"I DON'T LIKE CHOOSE YOUR OWN ADVENTURE® BOOKS. I *LOVE* THEM!" says Jessica Gordon, age 10. And now, kids between the ages of six and nine can choose their own adventure, too. Here's what kids have to say about the new Skylark Choose Your Own Adventure® books.

"These are my favorite books because you can pick whatever choice you want—and the story is all about you."
—**Katy Alson,** age 8

"I love finding out how my story will end."
—**Joss Williams,** age 9

"I like all the illustrations!"
—**Savitri Brightfield,** age 7

"A six-year-old friend and I have lots of fun making the decisions together."
—**Peggy Marcus** (adult)

Bantam Skylark Books in the Choose Your Own
   Adventure® Series
Ask your bookseller for the books you have missed

THE GENIE IN THE BOTTLE

JIM RAZZI

ILLUSTRATED BY KEVIN CALLAHAN

An R. A. Montgomery Book

A BANTAM SKYLARK® BOOK
TORONTO · NEW YORK · LONDON · SYDNEY

RL 2, 007–009

THE GENIE IN THE BOTTLE

A Bantam Skylark Book / June 1983

CHOOSE YOUR OWN ADVENTURE® *is a registered
trademark of Bantam Books, Inc.*

Original conception of Edward Packard.

*Skylark Books is a registered trademark of Bantam
Books, Inc. Registered in U.S. Patent and Trademark
Office and elsewhere.*

Front cover art by Paul Granger.

ISBN 0-553-15191-6

Published simultaneously in the United States and Canada

*Bantam Books are published by Bantam Books, Inc. Its trade-
mark, consisting of the words "Bantam Books" and the por-
trayal of a rooster, is Registered in U.S. Patent and Trademark Office and in other countries. Marca Registrada. Bantam
Books, Inc., 666 Fifth Avenue, New York, New York 10103.*

PRINTED IN THE UNITED STATES OF AMERICA

CW   0 9 8 7 6 5 4 3 2

This book is for my daughter,
Jenny Razzi

READ THIS FIRST!!!

Most books are about other people.

This book is about you—and your genie.

Genies are magic spirits trapped inside bottles or lamps. If you find a genie in a bottle and let him out, he will make your wishes come true.

Do not read this book from the first page through to the last page.

Instead, start at page one and read until you come to your first choice. Decide what you want to do. Then turn to the page shown and see what happens.

When you come to the end of a story, go back and try another choice. Every choice leads to a new adventure.

Genies have amazing magical powers. Anything can happen when you meet a genie. Good luck!

It's a cool autumn day, and you are walking along a deserted beach. Suddenly you see a strange-looking old bottle. It has been washed up by the sea.

You pick up the bottle and look at it closely. It is a dark golden color with a big cork stuck in the top. It is filled with smoke. Then in the smoke you see something. You look closer—the some*thing* is a some*one!* It's a tiny man. Could it be a genie?

Turn to page 2.

You can't believe your eyes. Are you dreaming? No! You've read all about genies. If you find one and let him out, he will grant your every wish.

Turn to page 4.

4   You are about to pull out the cork when you remember something else: there are good genies and bad genies. You wonder if the genie in *your* bottle is good or bad. There's only one way to find out—open the bottle.

But what if he's a bad genie? Maybe you should forget the whole thing and throw the bottle back into the ocean.

If you decide to open the bottle and let the genie out, turn to page 6.

If you decide to throw the bottle back, turn to page 15.

6   You decide to open the bottle and let the genie out. Using all your strength, you twist off the cork.

Pop! Who-o-o-sh!

A cloud of yellow smoke appears, and suddenly the genie is standing before you. He's nearly seven feet tall with *big* shoulders, but he's smiling at you. You decide he must be a good genie.

"Thank you for releasing me from the bottle," he booms. "Your *every* wish is my command."

Turn to page 8.

8   "*My* every wish is *your* command?" you ask.

"That is true," the genie replies.

"Great," you say, "but what should I wish for?"

"Wish for something you like," the genie tells you.

Hmmm, you just *love* pizza. Wouldn't it be great if everything you ate tasted like pizza?

But you also love to swim. You could wish that it were still summer. Then you could jump right into the water and swim to your heart's content.

If you wish that everything you eat tastes like pizza, go on to the next page.

If you'd rather take a swim, turn to page 13.

10   "Genie," you say, "I wish that everything I eat this week tastes like pizza."

Almost before you finish your sentence, you're sitting on a stool in Pete's Soda Shop. Boy, that genie works fast, you think.

You order a hamburger and french fries. They taste just like pizza! Then you order a soda. It tastes just like pizza, too.

On the way out, you buy an ice cream cone. Ugh! Pizza ice cream! You are beginning to think your wish was a mistake.

Turn to page 18.

"I want to go swimming," you say. The next thing you know, it's hot out and you're in your bathing suit. You dive into the water and start to swim. You are having so much fun that you don't realize you've swum out too far. When you look back, you don't think you can make it to shore.

"Help me, Genie!" you yell.

The genie looks worried. He yells back, "I wish I could help you, but I don't know how to swim. I'm sorry."

"*You're* sorry?" you shout. "What'll I do now?"

The genie rubs his head in thought.

"Well," he answers, "I could turn you into a fish, or I could throw you a rubber raft."

You have to think fast. What'll it be?

If you choose to become a fish, go on to the next page.

If you want the genie to throw you a rubber raft, turn to page 22.

14   "Quick, Genie, turn me into a fish," you sputter.

As soon as the words are out of your mouth, you find yourself swimming underwater.

The water feels cool as it flows past your gills. You swish your tail and little bubbles trail behind you. You're a great swimmer, and you move through the water with ease.

It's fun being a fish!

Turn to page 20.

You decide not to open the bottle—the genie inside could be a bad one. You fling it back out to sea. The bottle hits a rock and breaks open. Suddenly, in a puff of black smoke, you see a giant genie floating on the water. He starts swimming toward you. He looks mad!

Go on to the next page.

"So, you wouldn't let me out, would you?" he roars. "That makes me very angry!"

Uh-oh, you say to yourself, now I've done it. Your knees are knocking together overtime. Should you stand there and face the genie, or should you run away?

---

*If you decide to run away,
turn to page 26.*

*If you stay and face the genie,
turn to page 28.*

You take one last bounce and come to a stop. You lie down and take a deep breath. That was really fun! But the genie looks worried as he bounces over to you. "Are you all right?" he asks.

"Sure." You grin. "I always bounce back!" He laughs and asks you if you're ready to become you again.

"Not just yet," you say. "I think I'd like to be made of rubber a little while longer. Who knows? It might s-t-r-e-t-c-h my imagination!"

The genie chuckles as you both bounce down the street in search of new adventures. When you're made of rubber, there are lots of things you can do!

The End

18   You head for home feeling a little sick.

"Guess what we're having for supper tonight?" your mother says. "Your favorite food—*pizza*."

Your stomach does a somersault, and you start to turn green. And you still have six more days to go!

The End

20   You swim closer and closer to the bottom of the ocean. There is a huge rock in front of you. It's as big as a house. You have to swim around it.

If you swim to the left of the rock, turn to page 35.

If you swim to the right of the rock, turn to page 38.

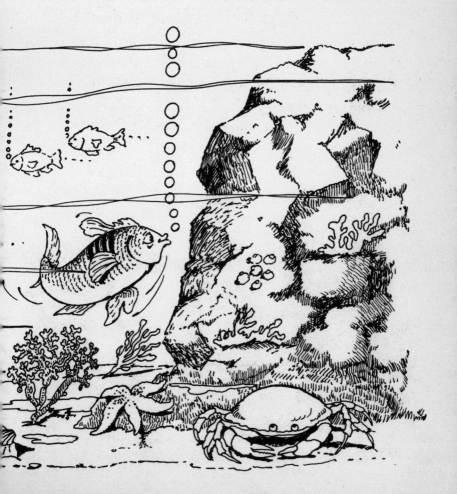

Your breath is giving out as you gasp, "Please, Genie, throw me a rubber raft."

You hear a swi-i-i-sh and a pop! Suddenly you're lying on a big rubber raft. You let out a sigh and lean back to rest.

Dreamily you stare up at the blue sky. You see a small plane circling above. It must be great to fly, you think. You figure you could do it. "I'll bet I could be as good as the Red Baron," you say aloud. "I wish I were flying his plane right now!"

No sooner are the words spoken than you find yourself and the genie in the Red Baron's triplane. You are at the controls.

Go on to the next page.

You fly over a small city and decide to show off. You start to loop and twist and spin. People look up, but instead of being impressed, they begin to shout: "It's a UFO!"

The Air Force thinks so, too. They send up a big jet fighter to check you out.

Will the fighter plane bring you down? You wonder if you should keep on flying.

If you keep on flying, turn to page 32.

If you decide to stop flying,
turn to page 31.

26 You start to run away from the genie. You look back, but the genie is nowhere in sight. You feel sure of yourself now.

"Ha," you laugh. "The big dummy's too slow to catch me!"

But when you turn to run down the beach, the genie is right in front of you.

How did he get *here*?

The genie frowns and waves his finger at you. Suddenly you're flat on your face in the sand. The genie has turned you into a sea turtle!

"Ha, ha," the genie roars. "Let's see how fast you can go now!"

You start to protest, but the genie has already disappeared. You shake your wrinkled head sadly. There's nowhere for you to go but to the sea. It's going to be your home from now on.

The End

You figure that it might be too dangerous to try to grab the flagpole. You could hurt your arm, even though it *is* made of rubber.

Then you notice that you are bouncing lower each time, like a real rubber ball.

Turn to page 17.

28   You decide to stay and see what happens. Besides, it wasn't your fault that the bottle broke.

The genie steps out of the water and looks at you. Suddenly he grins. "I admire courage," he roars. "I was just testing you.

"Now, even though you didn't release me on purpose, I'm grateful to be free. To show my thanks, I will grant you *one* wish."

You think fast. "I wish I could start all over again," you say.

"Okay," says the genie.

Turn to page 30.

30 You are holding a golden bottle. It looks sort of familiar. Inside the bottle you think you see a little man. Could it be a genie? You've read about them. If you release a genie from the bottle, it will grant your every wish.

But some genies are bad, and sometimes genies make bad wishes come true. Will this genie be good or bad?

Turn to page 4.

The fighter plane flies closer and starts to dive right at you. That does it! You've had enough flying for today. That safe sandy beach where you found the bottle seems so peaceful. Being back there would be nice. Having a quiet soda at Pete's Soda Shop sounds good, too. Anything is better than being chased by that jet.

You turn to the genie and make your next wish.

If you decide to go for a soda, turn to page 47.

If you would rather return to the sandy beach, turn to page 48.

32 You ignore your fears and decide to keep flying. The fighter plane comes closer. You do an upside-down loop to get out of its way. Just then, your seatbelt rips. You fall out of the plane, plunging through the air.

D
o
w
n

y
o
u

g
o
.
.
.

You are falling to earth faster and faster. The genie jumps out after you.

Go on to the next page.

"Quick, Genie," you shout. "I wish I could fly like a bird."

The genie looks worried. "I can't grant that wish," he says. "I forgot the magic words to make you fly like a bird. I can give you a parachute, though."

Go on to the next page.

You look down. There are tall buildings everywhere. You don't want to land *there*. But if you don't do something quickly, it will be too late.

You think as hard as you can. Then you get an idea! *Two* ideas, in fact. The first one is a little crazy and has to do with heights. The second one could really shake you up.

Which idea should you choose?

If you choose your first idea,
turn to page 36.

If you choose your second idea,
turn to page 42.

You swim around the left side of the rock and right into the biggest, meanest-looking shark you've ever seen. As he comes closer and closer, his huge mouth opens very wide. You can see his sharp teeth gleaming in the water. He is almost upon you. You realize too late that it's . . .

The End

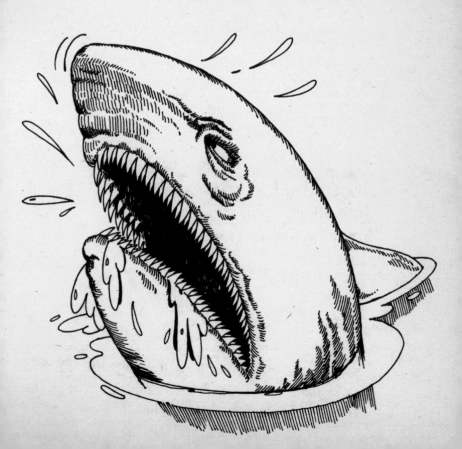

You decide your first idea is better.

"Genie," you ask, "can you make us fall up?"

The genie looks at you in surprise, then smiles.

"Not a bad idea," he says. Then he gestures with his hands and . . .

```
                                    !
                                 p
                                u


                            g
                          n
                         i
                        l
                       l
                      a
```

suddenly you find yourselves f

"It worked!" you shout.

You look down. The city is getting smaller and smaller.

Turn to page 44.

You swim around the right side of the rock, and suddenly you see a mermaid! You get so excited that you call to her and wave your tail.

"Hi, glub," you say, as the words bubble out of your mouth. "What's your, burble, name?"

"How cute," she says with a giggle, "a talking fish!" Then she tells you her name is Mirana. You tell her that you're really a human.

Turn to page 46.

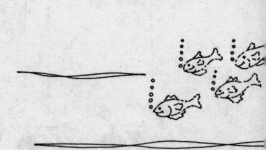

"Do you think you can stop us in time to land on the moon?" you ask the genie hopefully.

"Maybe," he answers, but he doesn't look too sure.

You look down at the earth again. It is now a small speck disappearing among the stars.

"Oh, well," you sigh. "I've always wanted to be an astronaut."

The End

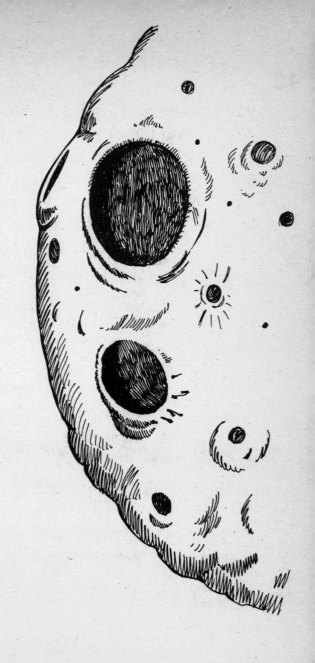

Your second idea is kind of tricky, but you're getting closer and closer to the ground, and there's no more time to think.

"Genie, I wish we were both made of rubber!"

At that moment you hit the ground. B-oi-oi-oing! You're in the air again. You've bounced! You're really made of rubber!

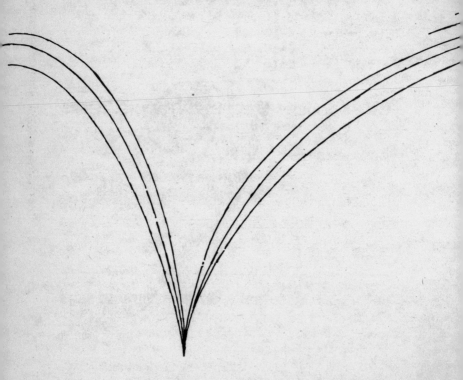

B-oi-oi-oing! You hit the ground again, and again you bounce up. You could go on like this forever.

On the way up, the third time, you spot a flagpole on a nearby building. Should you try to grab hold of it and stop? Or should you keep on bouncing?

If you try to grab the flagpole and stop, turn to page 52.

If you decide to keep bouncing, turn to page 27.

44   You fall higher and higher. You leave the earth's atmosphere.

You look down. The earth looks like a blue and white marble. You look up. The moon is getting closer and closer.

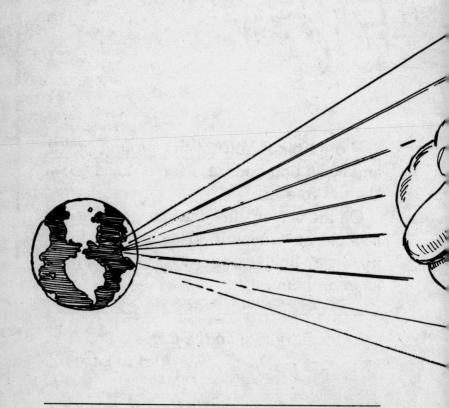

Turn to page 40.

"I've never, gulp, met a human before," she says.

"Well, I've never met a mermaid before," you answer.

You decide to remain a fish for a while. You and Mirana have a lot to talk about. You start to swim side by side, happily talking to each other.

"Wait until I tell my friends I talked to a human!" Mirana bubbles.

That's nothing, you think. Wait until the kids at school hear I talked to a mermaid!

The End

"Genie, I wish I could go to Pete's Soda Shop on Main Street."

As soon as you say it, you and the genie are on Main Street. The soda shop is across the street.

Suddenly you see Big Butch, the toughest kid in school, coming out the door. Butch has promised to give you a knuckle sandwich the next time he sees you. Maybe he's forgotten about it, or maybe he'll walk the other way.

But he sees you! He gives you a dirty look. Uh-oh! You turn to the genie for help, but he's already across the street.

Turn to page 50.

48   "I'd give anything to be back on that beach right now," you wish aloud.

"If I grant that wish, will you give me my freedom?" asks the genie.

You look at the jet again. It looks as if it means to knock you out of the sky.

"Yes!" you promise quickly.

The next thing you know, you're back on the beach. The plane and the genie are gone. All you hear is the quiet murmur of the waves.

You stand there for a moment, looking at the sea. Suddenly you see the genie in a boat, waving good-bye to you. You wave back with a smile. Having your own private genie was fun while it lasted.

The End

50   You have no choice. You swallow hard and cross the street.

Big Butch shakes his fist at you. He growls, "Oh, it's you, you twerp! Didn't I tell you I'd give you a knuckle sandwich the next time I saw you?"

You groan. You wish he had forgotten about all that.

Go on to the next page.

Suddenly, Big Butch smiles at you. "Hi there," he says. "Nice to see you again."

You wonder why Big Butch is being so nice. Then you realize what has happened. The genie has made him forget!

Butch is still smiling as he steers you inside the store and to the soda fountain. "Let me buy you an ice cream cone," he says, taking out his money.

You look over at the genie, and he winks at you. You smile back. It's going to be a great day after all.

The End

The flagpole is a little out of reach, but you try for it anyway, and your rubber arm s-t-r-e-t-c-h-e-s out and grabs the pole easily.

You climb in an office window, and a tall man comes over and shakes your hand.

"That was the best catch I've ever seen," he says. The man turns out to be the manager of your favorite baseball team.

"How would you like to be my star player?" he asks.

Turn to page 54.

54   You are thrilled. You've always wanted to be a baseball star. But what about the genie?

"I'd love to play ball for your team," you tell the manager, "but you have to hire a big, bald-headed batboy, too."

"Why not?" he agrees.

You lean out the window to tell the genie the good news. It's going to be an exciting baseball season!

The End

ABOUT THE AUTHOR

James Razzi is the bestselling author of numerous game, puzzle, and story books, including the Sherluck Bones Mystery-Detective and Slimy series. Well over two and a half million copies of his books have been sold in the United States, Britain, and Canada. One, *The Star Trek Puzzle Manual,* was on the *New York Times* bestseller list for a number of weeks. His fascinating book *Don't Open This Box!* was picked as one of the "Books of the Year" by the Child Study Association.

ABOUT THE ILLUSTRATOR

Kevin Callahan has been an illustrator for fifteen years. In addition to illustrating children's books and textbooks, he has worked in advertising. He is also the creator of a syndicated comic strip and the author of a book on antiques. His work has received awards from the Society of Illustrators and the Art Directors' Club. Mr. Callahan lives in Norwalk, Connecticut.

Now you can have your favorite Choose Your Own Adventure® Series in a variety of sizes. Along with the popular pocket size, Bantam has introduced the Choose Your Own Adventure® series in a Skylark edition and also in Hardcover.

Now not only do you get to decide on how you want your adventures to end, you also get to decide on what size you'd like to collect them in.

SKYLARK EDITIONS

☐	15120	The Circus #1 E. Packard	$1.75
☐	15207	The Haunted House #2 R. A. Montgomery	$1.95
☐	15208	Sunken Treasure #3 E. Packard	$1.95
☐	15149	Your Very Own Robot #4 R. A. Montgomery	$1.75
☐	15308	Gorga, The Space Monster #5 E. Packard	$1.95
☐	15309	The Green Slime #6 S. Saunders	$1.95
☐	15195	Help! You're Shrinking #5 E. Packard	$1.95
☐	15201	Indian Trail #8 R. A. Montgomery	$1.95
☐	15191	The Genie In the Bottle #10 J. Razzi	$1.95
☐	15222	The Big Foot Mystery #11 L. Sonberg	$1.95
☐	15223	The Creature From Millers Pond #12 S. Saunders	$1.95
☐	15226	Jungle Safari #13 E. Packard	$1.95
☐	15227	The Search For Champ #14 S. Gilligan	$1.95

HARDCOVER EDITIONS

☐	05018	Sunken Treasure E. Packard	$6.95
☐	05019	Your Very Own Robot R. A. Montgomery	$6.95
☐	05031	Gorga, The Space Monster #5 E. Packard	$7.95
☐	05032	Green Slime #6 S. Saunders	$7.95

Prices and availability subject to change without notice.

Buy them at your local bookstore or use this handy coupon for ordering:

Bantam Books, Inc., Dept. AVSK, 414 East Golf Road,
Des Plaines, Ill. 60016

Please send me the books I have checked above. I am enclosing
$_____ (please add $1.25 to cover postage and handling). Send check or money order—no cash or C.O.D.'s please.

Mr/Ms _____

Address _____

City/State _____ Zip _____

AVSK—11/83
Please allow four to six weeks for delivery. This offer expires 5/84.